The Black Bull
of Norroway

The Black Bull of Norroway

A SCOTTISH TALE
RETOLD BY
CHARLOTTE HUCK

PICTURES BY
ANITA LOBEL

Greenwillow Books
An Imprint of HarperCollins*Publishers*

The Black Bull of Norroway
Text copyright © 2001 by Charlotte S. Huck,
Trustee of the Charlotte S. Huck Living Trust,
dated October 22, 1992
Illustrations copyright © 2001 by Anita Lobel
All rights reserved.
Printed in Singapore by Tien Wah Press.
www.harperchildrens.com

Watercolor paints and a black pen were used to prepare the full-color art.
The text type is Original Garamond.

Library of Congress Cataloging-in-Publication Data
Huck, Charlotte S.
The Black Bull of Norroway: a Scottish tale / by Charlotte Huck;
illustrated by Anita Lobel.
p.   cm.
"Greenwillow Books."
Summary: A traditional Scottish tale set in Norway
in which a courageous girl sets out to seek her fortune
and ultimately finds true love.
ISBN 0-688-16900-7 (trade). ISBN 0-688-16901-5 (lib. bdg.)
[1. Fairy tales. 2. Folklore—Scotland.] I. Lobel, Anita, ill. II. Title.
PZ8.H862 Bl 2001   398.2'09411'02—dc21   [E]   00-034107

First Edition   10   9   8   7   6   5   4   3   2   1

To my sister Mary
for her loving and loyal support
— C. H.

Long ago in Norway there lived a widow with three daughters. One dark night the sisters began talking about marriage.

The eldest one said, "I will have no one lower than an earl. And he must own a beautiful castle."

The second one said, "I will have no one lower than a lord, and he must have a very large mansion."

Peggy Ann, the youngest and merriest, tossed her long braids and said, "I don't care what title he has or how wealthy he is. I only want him to be kind and good and to love me. I'd even be content with the Black Bull of Norroway."

Her sisters were horrified, for the Black Bull of Norroway was known to be a monster. But three times Peggy Ann repeated that she would be content with the Black Bull of Norroway.

Now the day came when the eldest daughter said to her mother, "Mother, bake me a bannock* and roast me a collop,** for I'm off to seek my fortune."

Her mother did so, and the daughter went to the wise woman. The wise woman told her to look out the back door and see what she could see. A coach with six horses was coming down the road.

"Well," said the wise woman, "that coach has come for you."

*A bannock is a flat cake made of oatmeal.   **A collop is a few slices of bacon or ham.

Soon after, the second daughter said to her mother, "Mother, bake me a bannock and roast me a collop, for I'm off to seek my fortune."

Her mother did so, and the girl went to see the wise woman. She, too, was told to look out the back door. This time a coach with four horses was coming down the road.

"That coach has come for you," said the wise woman.

Finally the day came when Peggy Ann asked her mother
to bake her a bannock and roast her a collop, for she was
off to seek her fortune.

"You, too, my youngest?" her mother said. But she gave
her the food and kissed her good-bye.

Peggy Ann went to see the wise woman and was told
to look out the back door. What she saw was a black bull
charging down the road. When he reached the house,
he stopped and waited.

"He's waiting for you," said the wise woman.

Peggy Ann was terrified. She remembered what she had
said about being content with the Black Bull of Norroway.

The wise woman took her out to the bull and helped her
climb on his broad back.

"Hold on to my horn with one hand," said the bull.
Slowly he trotted away.

They traveled on and on. Always the bull chose
the smoothest paths and easiest roads, until at last
Peggy Ann grew less afraid of him.

   After a time she became quite faint with hunger.
The bull spoke to her in a quiet voice saying,
"Eat out of my right ear and drink out of
my left ear and set aside whatever is left."
She did as he said and felt much better.

At last they arrived at a mysterious castle.

"This is where we will spend the night, for my eldest brother lives here," said the bull.

Servants came out and lifted Peggy Ann off the bull's back. They led the bull to a field and took Peggy Ann to the castle.

She was given a fine dinner and a soft bed on which to sleep. The next morning, when she was once again seated on the bull's back, the eldest brother gave Peggy Ann a gleaming red case in the shape of a round apple.

"Do not open the gold clasp," he said, "unless your heart is like to break and then to break again."

Peggy Ann and the bull traveled on, and always the bull chose the smoothest paths and the easiest roads. When they had traveled far, farther than the day before, they came in sight of another castle high on a hill.

"This is where we will spend the night," said the bull, "for my second brother lives here."

Many lords and ladies were guests at this castle. Peggy Ann and the bull were received cordially, just as they had been at the other brother's castle. When Peggy Ann was lifted from the bull's back this time, she asked that the bull be allowed to stay in the stable.

A magnificent banquet had been prepared, and later Peggy Ann was shown to a chamber with a huge bed surrounded by richly brocaded curtains.

In the morning the second brother presented Peggy Ann
with a golden case in the shape of a perfect pear.

"Do not open the gold clasp unless your heart is like to break
and then to break again," he told her.

Peggy Ann and the bull traveled on and on. The bull trod the
brambles underfoot and chose the smoothest paths, and Peggy
Ann ate out of his right ear and drank out of his left. The bull
grew tired and began limping. Just as the sun was setting,
they came to a smaller castle.

"Here we will stay," said the bull, "for my youngest
brother lives here."

The servants lifted Peggy Ann down. "Wait," she said. "I must look at the bull's feet to see why he limps."

She soon found a large thorn in one foot. The instant she pulled it out, the black bull vanished. In his place stood as handsome a young man as you're likely to see. He took Peggy Ann's hands in his and thanked her for breaking a cruel enchantment.

Now he could tell her that he was the Duke of Norroway. A wicked witch wanted him to marry her daughter. When he had refused, she had placed him under a spell. He would remain a bull until a beautiful maiden, of her own free will, did him a kindness, as Peggy Ann had just done.

"But the danger is not over," he quickly added. "Only at night am I myself. I have to conquer the Guardian of the Glen, and then the spell will be broken forever."

So the next morning the handsome Duke of Norroway was again a black bull, but Peggy Ann gladly climbed on his back.

Before they left, his youngest brother gave her a purple case in the shape of a round plum.

"Do not open the gold clasp unless your heart is like to break and then to break again," he said, and he wished them well.

And so they traveled on until they came to a dark and ugly glen surrounded by hills and mist-wrapped mountains.

The bull stopped and told Peggy Ann to
dismount and sit on a great rock.
"Here you must stay while I fight the Guardian
of the Glen," he said. "If everything around you
turns blue, you will know that I have beaten my
foe. But if all around you turns red, he will
have conquered me. But mind you do not
move a hand or a foot while I am away, or
I shall never find you again. "
And with a tremendous roaring bellow, the
bull set off to find the Guardian of the Glen.
Peggy Ann sat so still she hardly blinked.
She waited and waited and waited. Then
the mist rose, and everything around her
turned blue.
Peggy Ann was so overcome with
joy that she started to rise. She quickly
remembered and sat down, but it was
too late. The Duke of Norroway
searched and searched, but he
could not find her.

Peggy Ann sat and waited and waited and wept at her loss. The glen was dark except for one shining hill. If I could climb that hill, I could leave this glen, she thought. If the Duke of Norroway can't find me, perhaps I can find him.

But when she started to climb, she slipped and slipped and slid backward. She tried again and again, but it was as if the hill were made of glass.

Peggy Ann decided to try to walk around it. She walked until she came to a smithy.

The blacksmith promised her that if
she would work for him for seven years,
he would make her a pair of iron
shoes with spiked soles to help her
climb the glassy hill.
For seven years she cooked
and washed and swept and spun.
At the end of the seven long
years the blacksmith gave her
the iron shoes and told her
that the Duke of Norroway's
castle was just over the hill.

When Peggy Ann reached the other side of the hill, she came
to a cottage. Though she did not know it, the cottage belonged
to the witch who had cast the spell on the Duke of Norroway.
Now the witch was disguised as a washerwoman.

"It's a good thing you have come," she said to Peggy Ann.
"A handsome man left a bloody shirt here, and he promised
that whoever could wash it clean would be his bride. Both my
daughter and I have tried, but the stains only become worse.
Perhaps you can do it."

Peggy Ann did not know that the shirt belonged to her own
Duke of Norroway. She begged to lie down and rest, but the
washerwoman insisted that she wash the shirt first. The minute
Peggy Ann dipped it in the water, the shirt became sparkling
clean. "Now you can rest," said the washerwoman.

She and her daughter took the shirt to the castle, and the
washerwoman announced that her daughter had washed it.

The Duke groaned when he saw his bride-to-be, but he kept
his word and said he would marry her in three days.

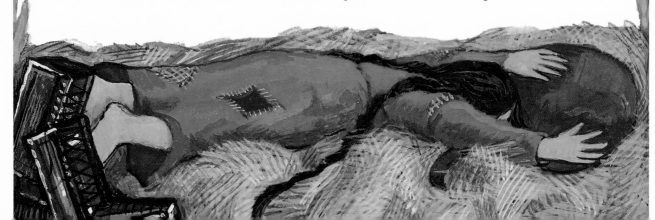

When Peggy Ann awoke, the washerwoman told her that the Duke of Norroway had agreed to marry her daughter. Peggy Ann's heart was like to break and then to break again.

She remembered her red apple case and took it from her bag. She opened the clasp and saw a necklace of beautiful pearls. The washerwoman's daughter asked her what she would take for them.

Peggy Ann quickly said, "They are not for sale, but I will give them to you if you let me sing outside the Duke's door tonight."

The daughter longed for the pearls, and she agreed to the trade. But she immediately went to her mother and asked her to prepare a sleeping potion that she could give to the Duke so he would not wake and hear Peggy Ann.

All through the long night Peggy Ann stood outside the Duke's door and sang and sobbed.

> "Seven long years I have worked for thee,
> The glassy hill I climbed for thee,
> The bloody shirt I washed for thee,
> Won't you come and speak to me?"

But the Duke could neither hear nor see her, and he slept the whole night through.

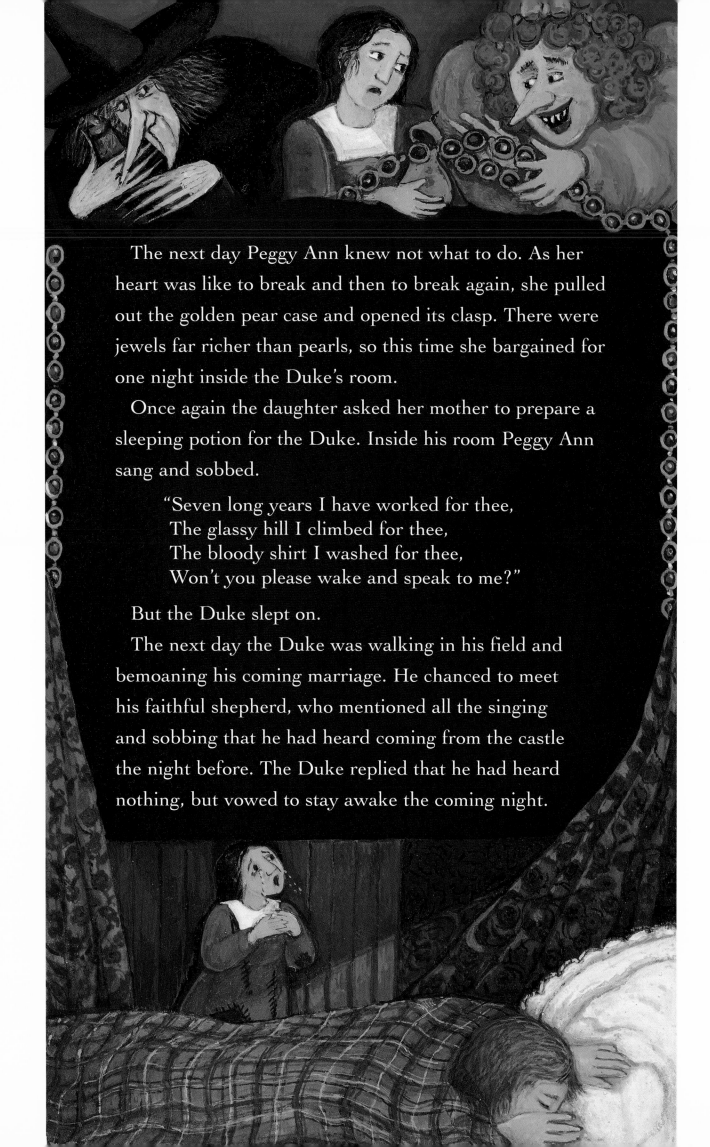

The next day Peggy Ann knew not what to do. As her heart was like to break and then to break again, she pulled out the golden pear case and opened its clasp. There were jewels far richer than pearls, so this time she bargained for one night inside the Duke's room.

Once again the daughter asked her mother to prepare a sleeping potion for the Duke. Inside his room Peggy Ann sang and sobbed.

"Seven long years I have worked for thee,
The glassy hill I climbed for thee,
The bloody shirt I washed for thee,
Won't you please wake and speak to me?"

But the Duke slept on.

The next day the Duke was walking in his field and bemoaning his coming marriage. He chanced to meet his faithful shepherd, who mentioned all the singing and sobbing that he had heard coming from the castle the night before. The Duke replied that he had heard nothing, but vowed to stay awake the coming night.

Peggy Ann was beside herself. Tomorrow was the Duke's wedding day. Once again her heart was like to break and to break again. She opened the purple plum case. She gasped at the brilliant diamond necklace inside. It was far more beautiful than the jewels of yesterday, and she easily bargained for one last night in the Duke's room.

This time when the washerwoman's daughter brought the Duke his sleeping potion, he asked her to fetch some honey to make it sweeter. While she was gone, he emptied the potion out the window and filled his mug with water from a pitcher.

When she returned with the honey, she put it in the water and watched him drink it. She left quite satisfied that he would again sleep the night through.

When Peggy Ann came into his room, the Duke appeared to be sound asleep. Quietly she made her way across the room, sat down at his side, and softly began to sing.

"Seven long years I have worked for thee,
The glassy hill I climbed for thee,
The bloody shirt I washed for thee,
Oh, dear Duke of Norroway,
Won't you turn and speak to me?"

The Duke sprang up and clasped her in his arms. Then Peggy Ann told him all that had happened to her, and he told her all that had happened to him. They agreed to be married the very next day.

When the witch washerwoman and her daughter realized that the Duke knew they had tricked him, they fled the country and were never seen again.

And the Duke of Norroway and his Peggy Ann lived happily ever after.

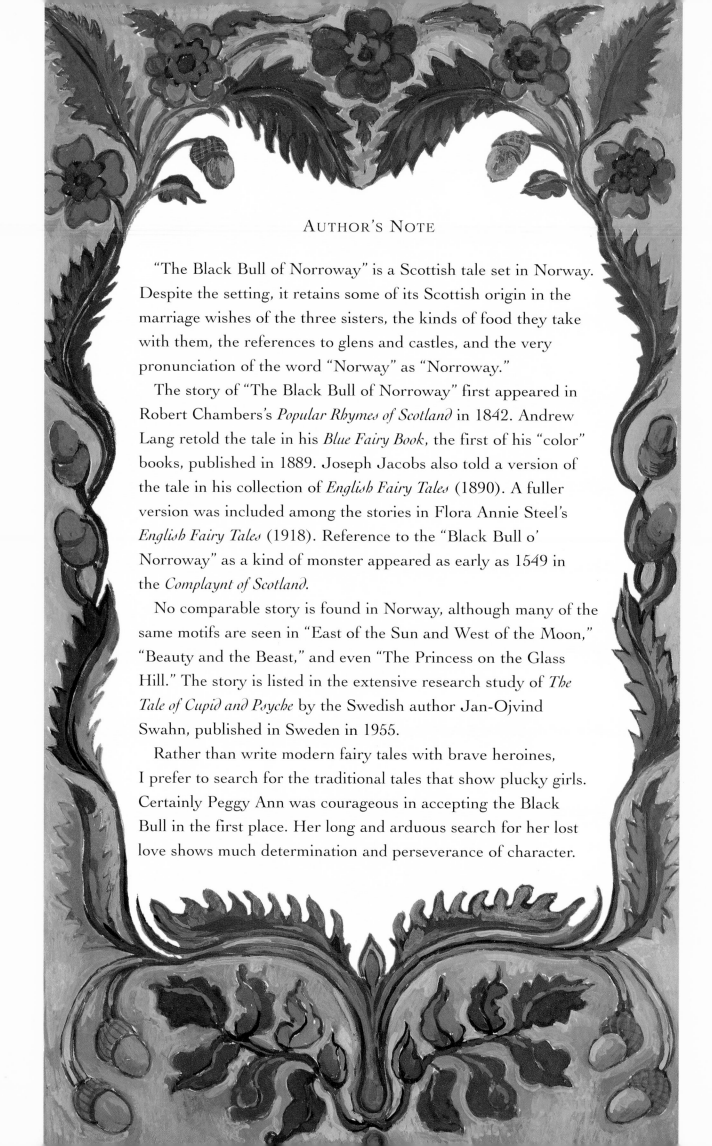

Author's Note

"The Black Bull of Norroway" is a Scottish tale set in Norway. Despite the setting, it retains some of its Scottish origin in the marriage wishes of the three sisters, the kinds of food they take with them, the references to glens and castles, and the very pronunciation of the word "Norway" as "Norroway."

The story of "The Black Bull of Norroway" first appeared in Robert Chambers's *Popular Rhymes of Scotland* in 1842. Andrew Lang retold the tale in his *Blue Fairy Book*, the first of his "color" books, published in 1889. Joseph Jacobs also told a version of the tale in his collection of *English Fairy Tales* (1890). A fuller version was included among the stories in Flora Annie Steel's *English Fairy Tales* (1918). Reference to the "Black Bull o' Norroway" as a kind of monster appeared as early as 1549 in the *Complaynt of Scotland*.

No comparable story is found in Norway, although many of the same motifs are seen in "East of the Sun and West of the Moon," "Beauty and the Beast," and even "The Princess on the Glass Hill." The story is listed in the extensive research study of *The Tale of Cupid and Psyche* by the Swedish author Jan-Ojvind Swahn, published in Sweden in 1955.

Rather than write modern fairy tales with brave heroines, I prefer to search for the traditional tales that show plucky girls. Certainly Peggy Ann was courageous in accepting the Black Bull in the first place. Her long and arduous search for her lost love shows much determination and perseverance of character.